MW01632661

The English Struwwelpeter

Heinrich Hoffmann

The English Struwwelpeter

Pretty Stories and Funny Pictures for Little Children

Bilingual Edition: English and German
Zweisprachige Ausgabe: Englisch und Deutsch

Die Bildvorlagen sind ausgewählten handkolorierten Struwwelpeter-Ausgaben des 19. Jahrhunderts entnommen (Sammlung Walter und Nadine Sauer, Neckarsteinach).

Third Edition

69239 Neckarsteinach (Germany)
www.editiontintenfass.de
info@editiontintenfass.de

Typesetting: τ-leχιs · O. Lange, Heidelberg
Printing and bookbinding: ADverts printing house, Riga (Latvia)

Printed in the European Union

ISBN 978-3-937467-54-2

Preface

Like *Mother Goose, Alice in Wonderland,* Grimms', Perrault's and Andersen's *Fairy Tales, Max und Moritz, Pinocchio,* and *Mickey Mouse,* Heinrich Hoffmann's *Der Struwwelpeter* is a world classic of children's literature. Never out of print after its first edition of 1845 and issued by numerous publishers, it has been a bestseller in Germany ever since. While few children in English speaking countries grow up with the book today, "Struwwelpeter" (or "Shock-headed Peter" or "Slovenly Peter") was a very familiar figure in their grandparents' and great-grandparents' nursery.

The first English version (of over twenty different ones), titled *The English Struwwelpeter,* was published in Leipzig in 1848. Although not a very close translation, it has remained by far the most popular and still has great appeal today. It is this version with its particular nineteenth century charm which we reissue here exactly 160 years after its first publication. The German original is found in the appendix. Also included below is a brief account by the author, "How I came to write Struwwelpeter," quaintly translated into English from the German original. It was contained in all English "copyright editions" of the book from the 1870's onwards and has become part and parcel of the "Struwwelpeter myth."

"How I came to write Struwwelpeter."

Doctor Heinrich Hoffmann, the author of Struwwelpeter, relates its origin as follows:

Towards Christmas in the year 1844, when my eldest son was three years old, I went to town with the intention to buy as a present for him a picture-book, which should be adapted to the little fellow's powers of comprehension. But what did I find? Long tales, stupid collections of pictures, moralizing stories, beginning and ending with admonitions like "the good child must be truthful," or: "children must keep clean", etc. But I lost all patience when I found a folio volume, where a bench, a chair, a jug, and many other things were drawn, and under each picture neatly written: "half, a third, or a tenth of the natural size". A child for whose amusement you are painting a bench, will think that a real bench; he has not and need not have an idea of the full size of a real bench. The child does not reason abstractedly, and the old tale of the bridge (vide: Gellert's celebrated German fable "the farmer and his son") will certainly impress him more than hundreds of general warnings like: "you must not tell stories".

That evening I nevertheless brought home a book, and handing it over to my wife, said: "there is what you wished for the little one". She took it, calling out rather amazed: "well that is a note-book with blank leaves". – "Just so, but we are going to make a book out of it". And it happened thus: I was then, although the medical man of the lunatic asylum, obliged to practice in town, where I was often brought in contact with children. Now, it certainly is a difficult thing for a Doctor to make little ones from 3 to 6 years old feel at ease with him because when they are in good health, the medical man and the chimney-sweep are very often made bugbears of. "My dear, if you are naughty the chimney-sweep will carry you off", or: "child, if you eat too much, the Doctor will come with his nasty medicine". The consequence is, that the little angel, when ill, begins to cry violently and to struggle as soon as the physician enters the room. An examination becomes utterly impossible, and the medical man cannot stay for hours vainly endeavouring to soothe the little patient. On such occasions a slip of paper and a pencil generally came to my assistance. A story, such as you find written here, invented on the spur of the moment, illustrated with a few touches of the pencil and humorously related, will calm the little antagonist, dry his tears and allow the medical man to do his duty.

In this manner most of the following absurd scenes originated. Some of them were later inventions, sketched in the same impulsive manner, without the least intention on my part of literary fame. The book was bound, put under the Christmas-tree, and the effect on the boy was just what I expected; not so, that produced upon some of my grown up friends who caught sight of my manuscript. From all sides I was asked to have it printed and published. I refused at first, as I had not the most distant idea of appearing before the public as author of juvenile story- and picture-books. But meeting one evening at a friend's house one of my present publishers, I was forced into it almost against my will, and thus the little home-bird flew into the wide, wide world, beginning, I may well say its voyage round the world. Shock-headed Peter, on his 31st birthday, celebrated his hundredth edition.

THE ENGLISH STRUWWELPETER
OR
PRETTY STORIES
AND
FUNNY PICTURES

When the children have been good,
That is, be it understood,
Good at meal-times, good at play,
Good all night and good all day –
They shall have the pretty things
Merry Christmas always brings.
Naughty, romping girls and boys
Tear their clothes and make a noise,
Spoil their pinafores and frocks,
And deserve no Christmas-box.
Such as these shall never look
At this pretty Picture-Book.

Just look at him! there he stands,
With his nasty hair and hands.
See! his nails are never cut;
They are grimed as black as soot;
And the sloven, I declare,
Never once has combed his hair;
Anything to me is sweeter
Than to see Shock-headed Peter.

Story of Cruel Frederick

Here is cruel Frederick, see!
A horrid wicked boy was he;
He caught the flies, poor little things,
And then tore off their tiny wings,
He killed the birds, and broke the chairs,
And threw the kitten down the stairs;
And oh! far worse than all beside,
He whipped his Mary, till she cried.

The trough was full, and faithful Tray
Came out to drink one sultry day;
He wagged his tail, and wet his lip,
When cruel Fred snatched up his whip,
And whipped poor Tray till he was sore,
And kicked and whipped him more and more:
At this, good Tray grew very red,
And growled, and bit him till he bled;
Then you should only have been by,
To see how Fred did scream and cry!

So Frederick had to go to bed;
His leg was very sore and red!
The Doctor came and shook his head,
And made a very great to-do,
And gave him nasty physic too.

But good dog Tray is happy now;
He has no time to say "Bow-wow!"
He seats himself in Frederick's chair
And laughs to see the nice things there:
The soup he swallows, sup by sup –
And eats the pies and puddings up.

Dreadful Story about Harriet and the Matches

It almost makes me cry to tell
What foolish Harriet befell.
Mamma and Nurse went out one day
And left her all alone at play;
Now, on the table close at hand,
A box of matches chanced to stand;
And kind Mamma and Nurse had told her,
That, if she touched them, they would scold her.
But Harriet said: "O, what a pity!
For, when they burn, it is so pretty;
They crackle so, and spit, and flame:
Mamma, too, often does the same."

The pussy-cats heard this,
And they began to hiss,
And stretch their claws,
And raise their paws;
"Me-ow" they said, "me-ow, me-o,
You'll burn to death, if you do so."

But Harriet would not take advice:
She lit a match, it was so nice!
It crackled so, it burned so clear –
Exactly like the picture here.
She jumped for joy and ran about
And was too pleased to put it out.

The pussy-cats saw this
And said: "Oh, naughty, naughty Miss!"
And stretched their claws,
And raised their paws:
"'Tis very, very wrong, you know,
Me-ow, me-o, me-ow, me-o,
You will be burnt, if you do so".

And see! oh, what a dreadful thing!
The fire has caught her apron-string;
Her apron burns, her arms, her hair –
She burns all over everywhere.

Then how the pussy-cats did mew –
What else, poor pussies, could they do?
They screamed for help, 'twas all in vain!
So then they said: "We'll scream again;
Make haste, make haste, me-ow, me-o,
She'll burn to death, we told her so."

So she was burnt, with all her clothes,
And arms, and hands, and eyes, and nose;
Till she had nothing more to lose
Except her little scarlet shoes;
And nothing else but these was found
Among her ashes on the ground.

And when the good cats sat beside
The smoking ashes, how they cried!
"Me-ow, me-oo, me-ow, me-oo,
What will Mamma and Nursey do?"
Their tears ran down their cheeks so fast,
They made a little pond at last.

Story of the Inky Boys

As he had often done before,
The woolly-headed Black-a-moor
One nice fine summer's day went out
To see the shops, and walk about;
And, as he found it hot, poor fellow,
He took with him his green umbrella.
Then Edward, little noisy wag,
Ran out and laughed, and waved his flag;
And William came in jacket trim,
And brought his wooden hoop with him;
And Arthur, too, snatched up his toys
And joined the other naughty boys;
So, one and all set up a roar,
And laughed and hooted more and more,
And kept on singing, – only think! –
"Oh! Blacky, you're as black as ink".

Now tall Agrippa lived close by –
So tall, he almost touched the sky;
He had a mighty inkstand too,
In which a great goose-feather grew;
He called out in an angry tone:
"Boys, leave the Black-a-moor alone!
For, if he tries with all his might,
He cannot change from black to white".
But ah! they did not mind a bit
What great Agrippa said of it;
But went on laughing, as before,
And hooting at the Black-a-moor.

Then great Agrippa foams with rage –
Look at him on this very page!
He seizes Arthur, seizes Ned,
Takes William by his little head;

And they may scream and kick and call,
Into the ink he dips them all;
Into the inkstand, one, two, three,
Till they are black, as black can be:
Turn over now, and you shall see.

See, there they are,
and there they run!
The Black-a-moor enjoys the fun.
They have been made as black as crows,
Quite black all over, eyes and nose,
And legs, and arms, and heads, and toes,
And trousers, pinafores, and toys –
The silly little inky boys!
Because they set up such a roar,
And teased the harmless black-a-moor.

Story of the Man that went out Shooting

This is the man that shoots the hares;
This is the coat he always wears:
With game-bag, powder-horn and gun
He's going out to have some fun.

He finds it hard, without a pair
Of spectacles, to shoot the hare.

The hare sits snug in leaves and grass,
And laughs to see the green man pass.

Now, as the sun grew very hot,
And he a heavy gun had got,
He lay down underneath a tree
And went to sleep, as you may see.
And, while he slept like any top,
The little hare came, hop, hop, hop,
Took gun and spectacles, and then
On her hind legs went off again.

The green man wakes and sees her place
The spectacles upon her face;
And now she's trying all she can,
To shoot the sleepy, green-coat man.
He cries and screams and runs away;
The hare runs after him all day
And hears him call out everywhere:
"Help! Fire! Help! The Hare! The Hare!"

At last he stumbled at the well,
Head over ears, and in he fell.
The hare stopped short, took aim, and hark!
Bang went the gun – she missed her mark!

The poor man's wife was drinking up
Her coffee in her coffee-cup;
The gun shot cup and saucer through;
"O dear!" cried she, "what shall I do?"
There lived close by the cottage there
The hare's own child, the little hare;
And while she stood upon her toes,
The coffee fell and burned her nose.
"O dear!" she cried, with spoon in hand,
"Such fun I do not understand."

Story of Little Suck-a-Thumb

One day Mamma said "Conrad dear,
I must go out and leave you here.
But mind now, Conrad, what I say,
Don't suck your thumb while I'm away.
The great tall tailor always comes
To little boys who suck their thumbs;
And ere they dream what he's about,
He take his great sharp scissors out,
And cuts their thumbs clean off – and then,
You know, they never grow again."

Mamma had scarcely turned her back,
The thumb was in, Alack! Alack!

The door flew open, in he ran,
The great, long, red-legged scissor-man.
Oh! children, see! the tailor's come
And caught out little Suck-a-Thumb.
Snip! Snap! Snip! the scissors go;
And Conrad cries out "Oh! Oh! Oh!"
Snip! Snap! Snip! They go so fast,
That both his thumbs are off at last.

Mamma comes home: there Conrad stands,
And looks quite sad, and shows his hands;
"Ah!" said Mamma "I knew he'd come
To naughty little Suck-a-Thumb."

Story of Augustus who Would not have any Soup

Augustus was a chubby lad;
Fat ruddy cheeks Augustus had:
And everybody saw with joy
The plump and hearty, healthy boy.
He ate and drank as he was told,
And never let his soup get cold.
But one day, one cold winter's day,
He screamed out "Take the soup away!
O take the nasty soup away!
I won't have any soup to-day."

Next day, now look, the picture shows
How lank and lean Augustus grows!
Yet, though he feels so weak and ill,
The naughty fellow cries out still
"Not any soup for me, I say:
O take the nasty soup away!
I won't have any soup to-day."

The third day comes; Oh what a sin!
To make himself so pale and thin.
Yet, when the soup is put on table,
He screams, as loud as he is able,
"Not any soup for me, I say:
O take the nasty soup away!
I WON'T have any soup to-day."

Look at him, now the fourth day's come!
He scarcely weighs a sugar-plum;
He's like a little bit of thread,
And, on the fifth day, he was – dead!

Story of Fidgety Philip

"Let me see if Philip can
Be a little gentleman;
Let me see, if he is able
To sit still for once at table":
Thus Papa bade Phil behave;
And Mamma looked very grave.
But fidgety Phil,
He won't sit still;
He wriggles,
And giggles,
And then, I declare,
Swings backwards and forwards,
And tilts up his chair,
Just like any rocking horse –
"Philip! I am getting cross!"

See the naughty, restless child
Growing still more rude and wild,
Till his chair falls over quite.
Philip screams with all his might,
Catches at the cloth, but then
That makes matters worse again.
Down upon the ground they fall,
Glasses, plates, knives, forks, and all.
How Mamma did fret and frown,
When she saw them tumbling down!
And Papa made such a face!
Philip is in sad disgrace.

Where is Philip, where is he?
Fairly covered up you see!
Cloth and all are lying on him;
He has pulled down all upon him.
What a terrible to-do!
Dishes, glasses, snapt in two!
Here a knife, and there a fork!
Philip, this is cruel work.
Table all so bare, and ah!
Poor Papa, and poor Mamma
Look quite cross, and wonder how
They shall have their dinner now.

Story of Johnny Head-in-Air

As he trudged along to school,
It was always Johnny's rule
To be looking at the sky
And the clouds that floated by;
But what just before him lay,
In his way,
Johnny never thought about;
So that every one cried out:
"Look at little Johnny there,
Little Johnny Head-in-Air!"

Running just in Johnny's way
Came a little dog one day;
Johnny's eyes were still astray
Up on high, in the sky;
And he never heard them cry:
"Johnny, mind, the dog is nigh!"
Bump! Dump!
Down they fell, with such a thump,
Dog and Johnny in a lump!

Once, with head as high as ever,
Johnny walked beside the river.
Johnny watched the swallows trying
Which was cleverest at flying.
Oh! what fun!
Johnny watched the bright round sun
Going in and coming out;
This was all he thought about.
So he strode on, only think!
To the river's very brink,
Where the bank was high and steep,
And the water very deep;
And the fishes, in a row,
Stared to see him coming so.

One step more! oh! sad to tell!
Headlong in poor Johnny fell.
And the fishes, in dismay,
Wagged their tails and swam away.

There lay Johnny on his face,
With his nice red writing-case;
But, as they were passing by,
Two strong men had heard him cry:
And, with sticks, these two strong men
Hooked poor Johnny out again.

Oh! you should have seen him shiver
When they pulled him from the rive
He was in a sorry plight!
Dripping wet, and such a fright!
Wet all over, everywhere,
Clothes, and arms, and face, and hai
Johnny never will forget
What it is to be so wet.

And the fishes, one, two, three,
Are come back again, you see;
Up they came the moment after,
To enjoy the fun and laughter.
Each popped out his little head.
And, to tease poor Johnny, said:
"Silly little Johnny, look,
You have lost your writing-book!"

Story of Flying Robert

When the rain comes tumbling down
In the country or the town,
All good little girls and boys
Stay at home and mind their toys.
Robert thought, "No, when it pours,
It is better out of doors."
Rain it *did*, and in a minute
Bob was in it.
Here you see him, silly fellow,
Underneath his red umbrella.

What a wind! oh! how it whistles.
Through the trees and flowers and thistles!
It has caught his red umbrella:
Now look at him, silly fellow –
Up he flies
To the skies.
No one heard his screams and cries;
Through the clouds the rude wind bore him,
And his hat flew on before him.

Soon they got to such a height,
They were nearly out of sight.
And the hat went up so high,
That it nearly touched the sky.
No one ever yet could tell
Where they stopped, or where they fell:
Only this one thing is plain,
Bob was never seen again!

Heinrich Hoffmann
Der Struwwelpeter
Lustige Geschichten und drollige Bilder

Vorspruch

Wenn die Kinder artig sind,
kommt zu ihnen das Christkind;
wenn sie ihre Suppe essen
und das Brot auch nicht vergessen,
wenn sie, ohne Lärm zu machen,
still sind bei den Siebensachen,
beim Spaziergehn auf den Gassen
von Mama sich führen lassen,
bringt es ihnen Gut's genug
und ein schönes Bilderbuch.

Der Struwwelpeter

Sieh einmal, hier steht er,
pfui! der Struwwelpeter!
An den Händen beiden
ließ er sich nicht schneiden
seine Nägel fast ein Jahr;
kämmen ließ er nicht sein Haar.
»Pfui!« ruft da ein jeder:
»Garstger Struwwelpeter!«

Die Geschichte vom bösen Friederich

Der Friederich, der Friederich,
das war ein arger Wüterich!
Er fing die Fliegen in dem Haus
und riss ihnen die Flügel aus.
Er schlug die Stühl und Vögel tot,
die Katzen litten große Not.
Und höre nur, wie bös er war:
Er peitschte seine Gretchen gar!

Am Brunnen stand ein großer Hund,
trank Wasser dort mit seinem Mund.
Da mit der Peitsch herzu sich schlich
der bitterböse Friederich;
und schlug den Hund, der heulte sehr,
und trat und schlug ihn immer mehr.
Da biss der Hund ihn in das Bein,
recht tief bis in das Blut hinein.
Der bitterböse Friederich,
der schrie und weinte bitterlich. –
Jedoch nach Hause lief der Hund
und trug die Peitsche in dem Mund.

Ins Bett muss Friedrich nun hinein,
litt vielen Schmerz an seinem Bein;
und der Herr Doktor sitzt dabei
und gibt ihm bittre Arzenei.

Der Hund an Friedrichs Tischchen saß,
wo er den großen Kuchen aß;
aß auch die gute Leberwurst
und trank den Wein für seinen Durst.
Die Peitsche hat er mitgebracht
und nimmt sie sorglich sehr in acht.

Die gar traurige Geschichte mit dem Feuerzeug

Paulinchen war allein zu Haus,
die Eltern waren beide aus.
Als sie nun durch das Zimmer sprang
mit leichtem Mut und Sing und Sang,

da sah sie plötzlich vor sich stehn
ein Feuerzeug, nett anzusehn.
»Ei«, sprach sie, »ei, wie schön und fein,
Das muss ein trefflich Spielzeug sein.
Ich zünde mir ein Hölzchen an,
wie's oft die Mutter hat getan.«

Und Minz und Maunz, die Katzen,
erheben ihre Tatzen.
Sie drohen mit den Pfoten:
»Der Vater hat's verboten!
Miau! Mio! Miau! Mio!
Lass stehn! Sonst brennst du lichterloh!«

Paulinchen hört die Katzen nicht!
Das Hölzchen brennt gar hell und licht,
das flackert lustig, knistert laut,
grad wie ihr's auf dem Bilde schaut.
Paulinchen aber freut sich sehr
und sprang im Zimmer hin und her.

Doch Minz und Maunz, die Katzen,
erheben ihre Tatzen.
Sie drohen mit den Pfoten:
»Die Mutter hat's verboten!
Miau! Mio! Miau! Mio!
Wirf's weg! Sonst brennst du lichterloh!«

Doch, weh! die Flamme fasst das Kleid,
die Schürze brennt; es leuchtet weit.
Es brennt die Hand, es brennt das Haar,
es brennt das ganze Kind sogar.

Und Minz und Maunz, die schreien
gar jämmerlich zu zweien:
»Herbei! Herbei! Wer hilft geschwind?
Im Feuer steht das ganze Kind!
Miau! Mio! Miau! Mio!
Zu Hilf! Das Kind brennt lichterloh!«

Verbrannt ist alles ganz und gar,
das arme Kind mit Haut und Haar;
ein Häuflein Asche blieb allein
und beide Schuh, so hübsch und fein.

Und Minz und Maunz, die kleinen,
die sitzen da und weinen:
»Miau! Mio! Miau! Mio!
Wo sind die armen Eltern? Wo?«
Und ihre Tränen fließen
wie's Bächlein auf den Wiesen.

Die Geschichte von den schwarzen Buben

Es ging spazieren vor dem Tor
ein kohlpechrabenschwarzer Mohr.
Die Sonne schien ihm aufs Gehirn,
da nahm er seinen Sonnenschirm.
Da kam der Ludwig hergerannt
und trug ein Fähnchen in der Hand.
Der Kaspar kam mit schnellem Schritt
und brachte seine Brezel mit;
und auch der Wilhelm war nicht steif
und brachte seinen runden Reif.
Die schrien und lachten alle drei,
als dort das Mohrchen ging vorbei,
weil es so schwarz wie Tinte sei!

Da kam der große Nikolas
mit seinem großen Tintenfass.
Der sprach: »Ihr Kinder, hört mir zu,
und lasst den Mohren hübsch in Ruh!
Was kann denn dieser Mohr dafür,
dass er so weiß nicht ist wie ihr?«
Die Buben aber folgten nicht
und lachten ihm ins Angesicht
und lachten ärger als zuvor
über den armen schwarzen Mohr.

Der Niklas wurde bös und wild, –
du siehst es hier auf diesem Bild!
Er packte gleich die Buben fest,
beim Arm, beim Kopf, bei Rock und West,
den Wilhelm und den Ludewig,
den Kaspar auch, der wehrte sich.
Er tunkt sie in die Tinte tief,
wie auch der Kaspar: »Feuer!« rief.
Bis übern Kopf ins Tintenfass
tunkt sie der große Nikolas.

Du siehst sie hier, wie schwarz sie sind,
viel schwärzer als das Mohrenkind!
Der Mohr voraus im Sonnenschein,
die Tintenbuben hintendrein;
und hätten sie nicht so gelacht,
hätt' Niklas sie nicht schwarz gemacht.

Die Geschichte vom wilden Jäger

Es zog der wilde Jägersmann
sein grasgrün neues Röcklein an;
nahm Ranzen, Pulverhorn und Flint
und lief hinaus ins Feld geschwind.

Er trug die Brille auf der Nas
und wollte schießen tot den Has.

Das Häschen sitzt im Blätterhaus
und lacht den blinden Jäger aus.

Jetzt schien die Sonne gar zu sehr,
da ward ihm sein Gewehr zu schwer.
Er legte sich ins grüne Gras;
das alles sah der kleine Has.
Und als der Jäger schnarcht' und schlief,
der Has ganz heimlich zu ihm lief
und nahm die Flint und auch die Brill
und schlich davon ganz leis und still.

Die Brille hat das Häschen jetzt
sich selber auf die Nas gesetzt,
und schießen will's aus dem Gewehr.
Der Jäger aber fürcht' sich sehr.
Er läuft davon und springt und schreit:
»Zu Hilf, ihr Leut! Zu Hilf, ihr Leut!«

Da kommt der wilde Jägersmann
zuletzt beim tiefen Brünnchen an.
Er springt hinein. Die Not war groß;
es schießt der Has die Flinte los.

Des Jägers Frau am Fenster saß
und trank aus ihrer Kaffeetass'.
Die schoss das Häschen ganz entzwei;
da rief die Frau: »O wei! O wei!«
Doch bei dem Brünnchen heimlich saß
des Häschens Kind, der kleine Has.
Der hockte da im grünen Gras;
dem floss der Kaffee auf die Nas.
Er schrie: »Wer hat mich da verbrannt?«
und hielt den Löffel in der Hand.

Die Geschichte vom Daumenlutscher

»Konrad!« sprach die Frau Mama,
»ich geh aus und du bleibst da.
Sei hübsch ordentlich und fromm,
bis nach Haus ich wieder komm.
Und vor allem, Konrad, hör!
lutsche nicht am Daumen mehr;
denn der Schneider mit der Scher
kommt sonst ganz geschwind daher,
und die Daumen schneidet er
ab, als ob Papier es wär.«

Fort geht nun die Mutter, und
wupp! den Daumen in den Mund.

Bautz! da geht die Türe auf,
und herein in schnellem Lauf
springt der Schneider in die Stub
zu dem Daumen-Lutscher-Bub.
Weh! Jetzt geht es klipp und klapp
mit der Scher die Daumen ab,
mit der großen scharfen Scher!
Hei! Da schreit der Konrad sehr.

Als die Mutter kommt nach Haus,
sieht der Konrad traurig aus.
Ohne Daumen steht er dort,
die sind alle beide fort.

Die Geschichte vom Suppen-Kaspar

Der Kaspar, der war kerngesund,
ein dicker Bub und kugelrund,
er hatte Backen rot und frisch;
die Suppe aß er hübsch bei Tisch.
Doch einmal fing er an zu schrein:
»Ich esse keine Suppe! Nein!
Ich esse meine Suppe nicht!
Nein, meine Suppe ess ich nicht!«

Am nächsten Tag, ja sieh nur her!
da war er schon viel magerer.
Da fing er wieder an zu schrein:
»Ich esse keine Suppe! Nein!
Ich esse meine Suppe nicht!
Nein, meine Suppe ess ich nicht!«

Am dritten Tag, o weh und ach!
wie ist der Kaspar dünn und schwach!
Doch als die Suppe kam herein,
gleich fing er wieder an zu schrein:
»Ich esse keine Suppe! Nein!
Ich esse meine Suppe nicht!
Nein, meine Suppe ess ich nicht!«

Am vierten Tage endlich gar
der Kaspar wie ein Fädchen war.
Er wog vielleicht ein halbes Lot, –
und war am fünften Tage tot.

Die Geschichte vom Zappel-Philipp

»Ob der Philipp heute still
wohl bei Tische sitzen will?«
Also sprach in ernstem Ton
der Papa zu seinem Sohn,
und die Mutter blickte stumm
auf dem ganzen Tisch herum.
Doch der Philipp hörte nicht,
was zu ihm der Vater spricht.

Er gaukelt
und schaukelt,
er trappelt
und zappelt
auf dem Stuhle hin und her.
»Philipp, das missfällt mir sehr!«

Seht, ihr lieben Kinder, seht,
wie's dem Philipp weiter geht!
Oben steht es auf dem Bild.
Seht! Er schaukelt gar zu wild,
bis der Stuhl nach hinten fällt;
da ist nichts mehr, was ihn hält;
nach dem Tischtuch greift er, schreit.
Doch was hilft's? Zu gleicher Zeit
fallen Teller, Flasch' und Brot,
Vater ist in großer Not,
und die Mutter blicket stumm
auf dem ganzen Tisch herum.

Nun ist Philipp ganz versteckt,
und der Tisch ist abgedeckt.
Was der Vater essen wollt,
unten auf der Erde rollt;
Suppe, Brot und alle Bissen,
alles ist herabgerissen;
Suppenschüssel ist entzwei,
und die Eltern stehn dabei.
Beide sind gar zornig sehr,
haben nichts zu essen mehr.

Die Geschichte vom Hans Guck-in-die-Luft

Wenn der Hans zur Schule ging,
stets sein Blick am Himmel hing.
Nach den Dächern, Wolken, Schwalben
schaut er aufwärts, allenthalben.
Vor die eignen Füße dicht,
ja, da sah der Bursche nicht,
also dass ein jeder ruft:
»Seht den Hans Guck-in-die-Luft!«

Kam ein Hund dahergerannt;
Hänslein blickte unverwandt
in die Luft.
Niemand ruft:
»Hans! gib acht, der Hund ist nah!«
Was geschah?
Pauz! Perdauz! – da liegen zwei!
Hund und Hänschen nebenbei.

Einst ging er an Ufers Rand
mit der Mappe in der Hand.
Nach dem blauen Himmel hoch
sah er, wo die Schwalbe flog,
also dass er kerzengrad
immer mehr zum Flusse trat.
Und die Fischlein in der Reih
sind erstaunt sehr, alle drei.

Noch ein Schritt! und plumps! der Hans
stürzt hinab kopfüber ganz! –
Die drei Fischlein sehr erschreckt
haben sich sogleich versteckt.

Doch zum Glück da kommen zwei
Männer aus der Näh herbei,
und die haben ihn mit Stangen
aus dem Wasser aufgefangen.

Seht! Nun steht er triefend nass!
Ei! das ist ein schlechter Spaß!
Wasser läuft dem armen Wicht
aus den Haaren ins Gesicht,
aus den Kleidern, von den Armen;
und es friert ihn zum Erbarmen.

Doch die Fischlein alle drei
schwimmen hurtig gleich herbei;
Strecken 's Köpflein aus der Flut,
lachen, dass man's hören tut,
lachen fort noch lange Zeit;
und die Mappe schwimmt schon weit.

Die Geschichte vom fliegenden Robert

Wenn der Regen niederbraust,
wenn der Sturm das Feld durchsaust,
bleiben Mädchen oder Buben
hübsch daheim in ihren Stuben. –
Robert aber dachte: »Nein!
Das muss draußen herrlich sein!« –
Und im Felde patschet er
mit dem Regenschirm umher.

Hui, wie pfeift der Sturm und keucht,
dass der Baum sich niederbeugt!
Seht! den Schirm erfasst der Wind,
und der Robert fliegt geschwind
durch die Luft so hoch, so weit.
Niemand hört ihn, wenn er schreit.
An die Wolken stößt er schon,
und der Hut fliegt auch davon.

Schirm und Robert fliegen dort
durch die Wolken immer fort.
Und der Hut fliegt weit voran,
stößt zuletzt am Himmel an.
Wo der Wind sie hingetragen,
ja! das weiß kein Mensch zu sagen.